WHITE WATER

Inspired by a true story

MICHAEL S. BANDY AND ERIC STEIN

ILLUSTRATED BY SHADRA STRICKLAND

CANDLEWICK PRESS

"Hurry up, Grandma," I said as I ran toward the bus stop. I didn't want us to miss the bus. We were going into town to get oats for the mule, and going to town was one of my favorite things.

We walked the six blocks to the bus stop. It was just a little bit past breakfast but already a thousand degrees outside. My feet were on fire, and my throat was as dry as a bone. It felt so good to sit down.

But before I could even catch my breath, we had to get up again.
Another boy and his mama had come to wait for the bus, too. Where we
lived, they could get to the stop last and still have first dibs on the bench.

They got on the bus first. They paid their fare and took
their seats. We got on the bus and paid our fare. Then we
got off the bus, walked to the back door, and got on the
bus again. Where we lived, that's how we did things.

I was so excited about going to town that I barely noticed how tired my legs were getting from standing so long. I saw the boy and his mama sitting in the front of the bus. I'd seen him at the bus stop before, so I waved at him. He smiled back at me.

By the time we finally got to town, I was really thirsty. I couldn't wait to run to the drinking fountain and take a big, long drink. I guess that other boy was thinking the same thing.

I was so thirsty that even the warm, rusty water tasted OK. But only for a few sips. After those first few sips, it tasted like nasty, muddy, gritty yuck.

It just didn't make any sense to me when that boy from the bus kept on drinking.

The water he was drinking must be cool. It must be fresh. I was sure it must be pure and icy cold, like mountain water. Suddenly I just had to know what that white water tasted like.

After the boy stopped drinking, I took a step in the direction of his fountain.

"Michael," my grandmother scolded, "don't you even think about doing anything like that." I stopped in my tracks.

But it was too late. The ideas were already flowing.

After that, I couldn't concentrate anywhere, not even at school. One moment I would be in class, then suddenly, I'd be crawling on my hands and knees in the hot desert. Out of nowhere, there was a palm tree with a water fountain under it. Above the fountain was a WHITES ONLY sign. I got up, opened my mouth, and was about to take a drink, when . . .

"Michael. Michael," the teacher said, "would you care to join us today?"

I snapped out of it. All the kids were laughing at me.

When I got home, I couldn't concentrate on my chores. I couldn't concentrate on eating. I couldn't even concentrate on taking a bath. All of a sudden, I was sitting in the middle of a giant water fountain. I had my arms open wide and my tongue out, ready to catch a drop.

"Michael. Michael!" my grandmother said. "You better not be getting any water on that floor."

That white water was starting to get me in trouble. That white water was all I could think about.

Later . . . I snuck into town and was standing in front of the fountain. I turned the knob, opened my mouth, and was about to take a big gulp. Then two big police officers grabbed me, hand-cuffed me, and said they were taking me to jail. I screamed, "Grandma! Grandma!"

"Wake up, boy," my grandmother said. "Sounds like you were having a bad dream."

Whew, I thought.

Wondering about that water was driving me crazy. I couldn't take it anymore. I just had to know what that white water tasted like. So I came up with a plan.

I'd go into town alone and get a taste of that white water.

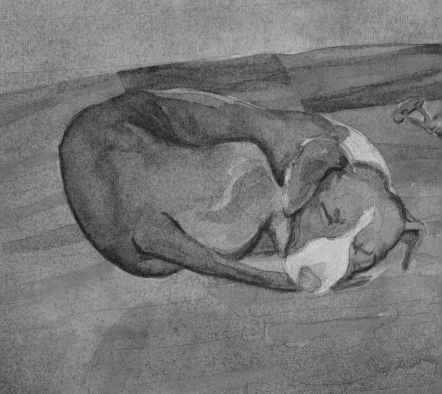

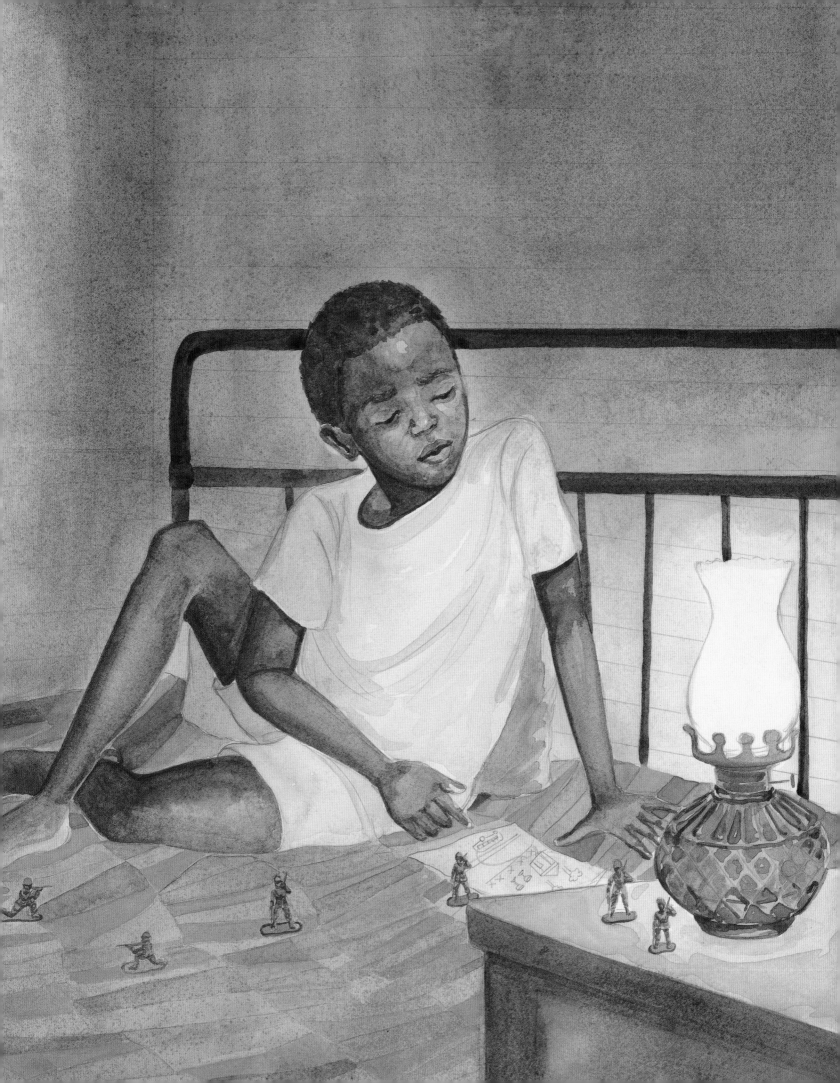

In *the morning*, I pretended I was sick. I waited till my grandmother went to work. If I got caught, she was going to be real mad, but I had to do it.

I walked down the road toward the bus stop with my dog, Shewee. Everyone who passed seemed to know I was up to no good.

When the bus driver asked me what I was doing riding alone, I told him I had missed the school bus. He just stared at me. I didn't know what to do, so I stared right back. He must've gotten tired of staring, because he finally pulled his hand off the coin slot.

When I *finally got to town,* I was scared to death. All kinds of things were running through my head. *What if I get caught? What if I get hurt? What if they put me in jail forever?* But I just had to know what that white water tasted like.

I looked both ways. The coast was clear.

I took a deep breath and ran toward the bus depot.

I ran as fast as I could, and I swear I could hear my grandmother's voice saying, "I got you covered. Now, go for it."

There was no turning back now. This was it.

I took a big gulp. That white water wasn't cool. That white water wasn't fresh. That white water wasn't pure and icy cold, like mountain water. It tasted like nasty, muddy, gritty yuck, just like our water.

Then suddenly she appeared. That lady. The one with the boy. But today she was alone. "Boy, you know you don't belong here!" she shouted.

I was startled and fell down. I was so frightened, I couldn't hear what she was saying. Lying on the ground, all I could see was the pipe. I'd never seen it from that angle before. The same pipe fed both fountains! Two fountains. Two signs. But the same water in both!

The signs over the fountains had put a bad idea in my head. But they were a lie. If they weren't real, what else should I question? Maybe there were lots of things—like that nasty old white water—that weren't true. That had nothing to do with nothing. Maybe everything I thought I couldn't do was just in my imagination, too. That's when I realized— I could do anything.

   Now I knew. And from that day on, I wouldn't let anything stand in my way.

Authors' Note

This story is a work of our imaginations but is inspired by the true experiences of Michael Bandy's childhood. His wonderful grandmother, his dog, his home, and the prejudice of the world he lived in as a boy were all real. But some of the other barriers he faced were actually the self-doubt he created in his mind. What we learned from our childhoods is that by embracing the gifts of imagination and courage, we can blast beyond the impossible and ultimately achieve anything.

THANKS TO

Dennis Hackin, Spencer Humphrey, Ed Labowitz, Pam Consolazio, Nicole Raymond, and Karen Lotz

For my mom, Annie Bandy
M. S. B.

For my dad, B. E. Stein, MD
E. S.

For my grandmother, Ruth, who makes me smile
S. S.

Text copyright © 2011 by Michael S. Bandy and Eric Stein
Illustrations copyright © 2011 by Shadra Strickland

First paperback edition 2015

Library of Congress Cataloging-in-Publication Data

Bandy, Michael S.
White water / Michael S. Bandy and Eric Stein ; illustrated by Shadra Strickland. — 1st U.S. ed.
p. cm.
Summary: After tasting the warm, rusty water from the fountain designated for African Americans,
a young boy questions why he cannot drink the cool, refreshing water from the "Whites Only" fountain.
Based on a true experience co-author Michael S. Bandy had as a boy.
ISBN 978-0-7636-3678-4 (hardcover)
[1. Segregation — Fiction. 2. African Americans — Fiction.] I. Stein, Eric, date. II. Strickland, Shadra, ill. III. Title.

PZ7.B22125Wh 2011
[E] — dc22   2010040343

ISBN 978-0-7636-7945-3 (paperback)

19 20 APS 10 9 8 7

Printed in Humen, Dongguan, China

This book was typeset in Dante.
The illustrations were done in watercolor, ink, and gouache.

Candlewick Press
99 Dover Street
Somerville, Massachusetts 02144

visit us at www.candlewick.com